THE STORIES

Aeneas and Dido

In this ancient Greek ghostly tale, the hero journeys to the underworld.

Aeneas, hero of the defeated Trojans, escaped the destruction of Troy with his father and a group of followers. The gods had decided that his fate was to found a settlement in Italy whose descendants would become the first Romans.

On his long journey, Aeneas's father died on the island of Sicily. After six years of looking for a suitable place to start his settlement, Aeneas was blown off course by a terrible storm. He and his followers ended up in Carthage on the north coast of Africa. There he met Dido, the beautiful Queen of Carthage.

Aeneas fell in love with Dido and spent a year helping her to improve the city. There were plans for them to marry, but the gods sent a message to Aeneas telling him to leave.

Aeneas secretly left Carthage with his followers. When Dido realized he had left, her heart was broken and she killed herself.

A coin was placed in a dead person's mouth to pay Charon, the ferryman.

Aeneas eventually made landfall on the coast of Italy. It was there he was to meet his dead father in the underworld to learn about the future. He traveled to the Temple of Apollo, and met the **Sibyl**. The priestess guided Aeneas into the underworld, where Charon ferried them across the Acheron.

Passing through the Fields of Mourning, where those who died for love wander, Aeneas came across Dido. Saddened, he spoke to her, claiming that he had not left her of his own free will. The shadow of the dead queen ignored him, turning away from her beloved. Aeneas shed tears of pity.

The Ghost of Temessa

This ancient Greek ghost story is about a very violent and dangerous ghost.

During his ten years of wandering, the hero Odysseus arrived at the town of Temessa. Before he continued homeward, one of the ships' crew attacked a young woman. Odysseus left him to his fate and the culprit was captured and stoned to death by the town's people.

Not long after, the people were set upon by the dead man's ghost. Men and women were killed as the ghost took his vengeance on the frightened inhabitants. They sought the advice of the town's **Pythian priestess** who told them to build a temple to the dead man and sacrifice a young maiden to him once a year. This they did and the ghostly attacks stopped.

*Odysseus was a hero of the **Trojan War**. He had many adventures on his journey home to Ithaca. On one occasion, he avoided being shipwrecked by **sirens** by having his men stuff their ears with beeswax. He was able to listen to their song while tied to the ship's mast.*

One year, the famous wrestler and boxer Euthymus arrived in town on the day the people were making the annual sacrifice. On hearing how matters stood, he went to meet the young maiden who was to be sacrificed and immediately fell in love with her. The girl swore to be his wife if he could save her. So Euthymus waited with her for the spirit to arrive.

As the ghost appeared and saw Euthymus, it let out a terrifying scream and launched a fearful attack on the young wrestler. Although it was vicious and cunning, the ghost was no match for Euthymus, who threw its battered body into the sea.

The wedding was celebrated by the entire town and the ghost was never seen again.

Haunted House

This original haunted house story was recorded by the ancient Roman, Pliny the Younger.

One day, long ago, the philosopher Athenodorus arrived in Athens looking for a place to live. He came across a large house that seemed to have been deserted for some time.

Making enquiries, he discovered that the house was

Pliny the Younger was a lawyer, author, and magistrate of ancient Rome. Along with his father, he was a witness to the eruption of Vesuvius in 79 AD.

haunted. No one, not even the agent, held back the horrific details. "People have died of fright there!" he said. "They say you hear the rattling of chains. Then a horrible vision appears of a filthy old man in rags, weighed down by chains."

Despite the warnings, the philosopher decided to buy the building. On the very first night in the haunted house, Athenodorus gave the servants the night off. Then he sat down at a table with stylus and paper and, in the glow of a lantern, began to write.

At first, all was quiet. Then a faint noise of the scrape and clank of chains was heard. Athenodorus kept his head down and continued to write. The sounds grew louder and louder until they seemed to be coming from the very room he was in.

Athenodorus put down his stylus and looked up. There in front of him was a ghastly vision. The shadow of an old man with wisps of hair and sunken eyes stared back at him. His filthy rags were bound with broken chains.

The shadow beckoned Athenodorus and, as the philosopher got up, the ghost shambled off toward an open area in the house. As Athenodorus approached the shadow, it disappeared.

The next morning, Athenodorus had his servants dig up the ground where the shadow had disappeared. There they discovered the decayed remains of a tortured man in chains. The remains were given a proper burial and the shadow was never seen again.

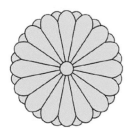

O-Sono's Ghost

This famous ghost story, based on a Japanese folk tale, explains why some ghosts appear to us.

A long time ago, the daughter of a rich merchant of Tamba was sent to Kyoto to be educated. Her name was O-Sono. After her education, she returned home and was married to a merchant named Nagaraya.

She lived happily with her husband and had one child. But, after four years, she became ill and died. On the night after her funeral her son approached his father and told him that his mother was in the bedroom. He had tried to speak with her but had become afraid as she would not answer him.

When Nagaraya entered the bedroom, he was shocked to see an apparition of his wife. She was sitting, and staring with a concerned expression in the direction of a chest of drawers. They still contained some of her clothes and jewelry. Frightened, Nagaraya backed out of the room with his son. When Nagaraya told his mother, she said, "Maybe she has come back to look at her things. The dead do that sometimes. Empty the drawers and take them to the temple."

Nagaraya took the clothes and jewelry to the temple, but his wife's ghost kept appearing every night. Eventually, he told the parish priest about O-Sono. The priest suggested that he come to the house to speak to her.

The priest waited alone and, when O-Sono materialized, the priest said, "I have come here to help you." He searched the empty drawers thoroughly and under the paper lining he found a letter. It was a love letter written to her when she was in Kyoto. The priest told no one and burnt the letter. After that, the ghostly apparition of O-Sono never appeared again.

In Japanese folktales ghosts are called "yūrei."

Blackfoot Ghosts

This ghost story from North America warns against taking things left behind by ghosts.

A long time ago, a small band of Blackfoot warriors went on a war party. They traveled a great distance until their horses could go no farther. When the last horse died, they decided to return home.

As they passed through the Sand Hills, they saw fresh trails where a large group of people had been traveling. They decided to follow the trail since it was likely that they were made by their own people. Suddenly, one of them stopped.

"Look! This is a stone hammer that belonged to my mother," he said. "How can this be? It was buried with her when she died." The warriors were not sure what to make of it but, as night was almost upon them, they decided to pitch camp.

The Blackfeet were nomadic bison hunters who ranged across the northern Great Plains of North America.

In the morning, the warriors were woken by the sound of many people. But, when they looked around, they saw nothing and became afraid. When the sounds died down, their courage returned and they began to search the area.

Soon, one of them found an arrow that was painted red. "This belonged to my father!" he exclaimed.

Another caught sight of his father chasing and killing a buffalo but, when they drew near, the father and buffalo disappeared. Other objects that were familiar to them were collected by the warriors.

Eventually, the warriors left and made their way home. The one who had collected the hammer died as soon as he got back. Two of the others were killed soon afterward. It seemed that the ghosts who owned the items were angry and had followed them back to their homes and killed them.

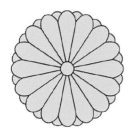

The Ghost of Okiku

This is a Japanese story of how a ghost got its revenge on its killer.

There was once a maid called Okiku who worked for a samurai named Tessan Aoyama. This high-born nobleman fell in love with the pretty, young maid and asked her to marry him. But Okiku did not find him attractive and spurned his advances.

Aoyama became enraged at Okiku's rejection. "How can a simple maid reject a nobleman like me?" he asked himself. After several attempts to change her mind, Aoyama came up with a plan. It was the maid's duty to clean the ten plates of his precious collection. One night, he crept downstairs and broke one of the plates.

In the morning, the maid discovered the smashed plate and shrieked in horror. She cleaned up the pieces and hid them. She knew she would be blamed for the breakage and thought only of escaping the wrath of her employer.

When Aoyama appeared minutes later, he pointed to his plate collection and started counting, "One, two, three, four... where is the tenth plate?"

Okiku stood staring at the floor, trembling.

"I will not punish you if you agree to marry me," declared Aoyama. But Okiku still refused. In a fit of rage, the samurai grabbed the maid and killed her on the spot. He took her body outside and threw it down the well.

That night, Aoyama was woken by a strange wailing. He made his way to the source of the noise, which seemed to be coming from the well. Suddenly, the ghost of Okiku appeared, floating out from the well. "One, two, three... ," she counted. When she got to nine, she let out a terrifying scream. Each night, the ghost appeared, counting, until it drove Aoyama to complete madness.

In Japan, it is believed the misplaced souls of people who have not been buried properly sometimes become vengeful ghosts called "onryō."

Ghost Ship

This is the story of what happened to the ghost ship Lady Lovibond.

In 1798, several different ships' captains reported seeing a ship in distress on the notorious Goodwin Sands off the south-east coast of England. It was the phantom ship *Lady Lovibond*. Fifty years later, lifeboats were sent out to look for survivors from the same ship, in trouble on the treacherous sands.

The ghost ship kept appearing every 50 years. The last sighting was in 1948. The reason the ghostly apparition kept returning might be because of the sad tale of the ship's last voyage.

The schooner was at sea on February 13, 1748, bound for Oporto in Portugal. The captain Simon Reed had recently married and he was taking his bride Annette on a honeymoon cruise. There was a longstanding superstition among sailors that it was bad luck to allow a woman on board. The sailors, however, were happy to have her along and were celebrating the marriage below deck. All, that is, except one man—the first mate John Rivers.

John Rivers had been a rival for the hand of the captain's young wife. He paced the deck of the *Lady Lovibond*, steadily growing more and more angry.

Suddenly, seized by a fit of jealous rage, he picked up a club-like belaying pin and hit the sailor at the wheel, knocking him unconscious. Seizing the wheel, the jealous Rivers steered the schooner onto the Goodwin Sands. All on board were drowned as the ship broke up and sank beneath the waves.

The most famous ghost ship is the Flying Dutchman. This oceanic specter can never make port and is doomed to sail the oceans forever. The sight of the ship means impending doom.

Headless Horseman

This is a retelling of a folktale on which Washington Irving based his famous ghost story, The Legend of Sleepy Hollow.

One dark night, a Dutchman left the tavern in Tarrytown and started to make his way home to the village nearby. His route took him past the old Sleepy Hollow graveyard.

He whistled nervously to keep his courage up. He had heard stories in the tavern about ghostly apparitions. It was in that graveyard that the headless corpse of a **Hessian soldier** had been buried during the **American Revolutionary Wa**r.

Suddenly, out of the corner of his eye, he saw something move. His heart pounded in his chest as he watched mist rise from a grave. It quickly formed into the ghostly figure of a headless man, mounted on a horse.

The Dutchman let out a horrified scream and ran for his life. Behind him, he could hear the terrifying whinny of the horse as its ghoulish rider spurred it on.

The Dutchman ran as fast as he could, heading for a small bridge that spanned a stream. He knew that ghosts and evil spirits could not travel over flowing water.

In his haste, he stumbled and fell, rolling down from the side of the road and under a bush. The headless rider galloped past and, as it did so, the Dutchman saw that it was wearing the uniform of a Hessian soldier.

The next day, the Dutchman told his story to the people of Tarrytown. They all agreed that it was the very same ghost of the Hessian soldier who had lost his head in a battle nearby.

In Irish mythology, a headless rider is known as a dullahan. It usually carries its head under its arm and uses a human spine as a whip!

Banshee

This hair-raising story from Irish mythology is about an omen of death.

In Ireland in 1776, in the parish of Kilchreest, the Ross-Lewin children were returning from an evening's entertainment at a friend's house. It was a warm night and, since their father had been called away on business in Dublin, there was no rush to get home quickly.

As they neared the ruined church, they heard the wailing and hand clapping of a person lamenting the dead. When they came up to the edge of the graveyard, they saw an old woman with gray hair against the ruined walls of the old church. She was running up and down, chanting and waving her arms in the air.

As soon as the young men rushed into the church graveyard, the old woman disappeared. They looked inside the building and all over the church grounds, but she was nowhere to be seen. They were truly frightened and rushed back home to their mother.

When they reached home, their mother opened the door. She had been waiting for them anxiously and told them about a raven that had tapped on the windows. When they told her about the banshee they had seen, she became very worried that something may have happened to their father. Suddenly, there were taps again on the window. The raven had returned and they all saw it staring into the room with its beady, black eyes before it flew off into the night.

A few days later, news reached them that Mr Ross-Lewin had died in Dublin. It seemed that the banshee had indeed foretold his death.

Banshees may also appear not only as a woman, a raven, or a hooded crow, but as a stoat, a hare, or a weasel.

A Ghostly Warning

A ghostly sight has future consequences
for Lord Dufferin in this tale from Ireland.

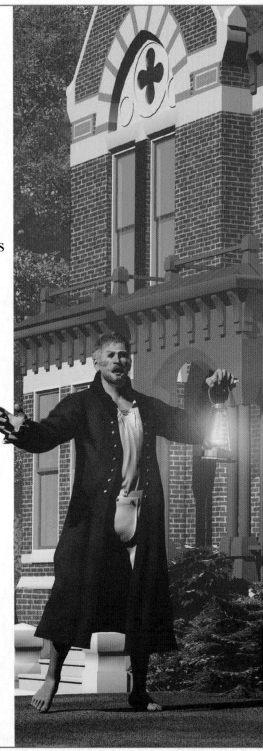

In 1879, Lord Dufferin, the British ambassador to France, was on vacation with a friend in Ireland. One night, he awoke from an uneasy sleep and heard footsteps in the garden below. Looking out from his bedroom window, he saw a figure carrying a coffin on his back.

Lord Dufferin lit a lamp and made his way down the stairs and out into the garden. He approached the figure and demanded to know what he was doing.

"You're trespassing on private property," he said. The figure turned to face him and Lord Dufferin stepped back in shock. Staring at him was a face with the sunken cheeks and ghastly grin of a corpse. Its shriveled body had ancient leathery skin. The figure turned without a word and walked away. It turned into mist, then vanished.

The next morning Lord Dufferin shared the tale of his encounter with his host who could shed no light on the event, as there had been no previous sightings of ghosts.

Four years later, Lord Dufferin attended a party at the Grand Hotel in Paris. He was about to step into the elevator, when he suddenly spotted the terrifying figure from Ireland, dressed as the elevator operator. Lord Dufferin stepped back as the doors closed. The elevator rose, but then came the sound of snapping cables. The elevator plummeted to the ground, killing all those inside.

It was discovered later that the hotel's usual elevator operator had not reported for work that day.

The ancient Greek poet Simonides said that he was saved from certain death by seeing the ghosts of the twin gods Castor and Pollux.

GLOSSARY

American Revolutionary War Fought between 1775 and 1783, it was the successful military rebellion against Great Britain by the Thirteen American Colonies that became the United States of America in July 1776.

Hessian soldier German soldiers employed by the British during the American War of Independence.

Pythian priestess A priestess who belonged to the temple of Apollo at Delphi. Pythia was the original name for Delphi.

Sibyl In ancient Greek mythology, a woman believed to have the gift of foretelling the future.

Siren An ancient Greek mythical creature with the body of a bird and the head of a woman. Sirens lured sailors to their death with their beautiful singing.

Trojan War In Greek mythology, a war waged against the city of Troy by the Greeks after Paris of Troy took Helen from her husband Menelaus, the king of Sparta.

INDEX